Dedicated to my wonderful
friend, Dorothea Majerczyk.

God bless!

Dorothea's love for dogs started when she was about the age of fourteen. Her parents invited all her friends from the neighborhood to her birthday party. There were plenty of games and a big cake with fourteen candles burning bright.

Dorothea's mom had always wanted to own a dog, but she knew that pets need plenty of attention and lots of care. With Dorothea getting older, it seemed the time was right for a puppy. After all, a dog would bring so much joy to their family.

During the party, Dorothea thought she heard a puppy barking. Her mother just smiled and kissed her cheek. As Dorothea blew out the candles, she made a wish, never thinking that it might come true. But at that moment, her father walked into the room carrying the cutest puppy ever.

Dorothea shouted, "That's my wish! That's my wish!"

Everyone at the party wanted to hold and touch the puppy. One friend asked, "What's his name?"

Dorothea replied, "I don't know."

Dorothea's mother said, "We haven't given him a name yet because it's up to Dorothea to name him."

When the party ended, the puppy followed Dorothea around for the rest of the day. When she stopped walking he would run into the back of her legs. She felt his little wet nose and he'd let out a little yelp.

Her mother said, "He's like a shadow behind you."

"Thanks for that name mom," Dorothea said. "From now on his name will be Shadow."

Shadow was a bit of a handful because he loved chewing up everything in sight. All of Dorothea's shoes were filled with bite marks, but she didn't want to tell her Mom. After all, Dorothea wanted to keep Shadow out of trouble.

Something needed to be done, but Dorothea didn't know what. She would pet Shadow and talk softly, saying, "Don't bite anymore."

He would only look up at her and let out a small bark before jumping all over her. Dorothea knew she needed to figure out a way to train her puppy fast.

The next day, she asked her mom if they could visit the library. Sure enough, she found book after book about dog training. Dorothea took a few of the books home and read aloud to Shadow, even though he wouldn't understand. But the more she worked with him, the smarter Shadow became. As time passed, he was not only trained, he was the best dog in the neighborhood!

Dorothea and Shadow became best friends. Sometimes on their walks she noticed dogs roaming around by themselves without chains, collars, or tags. Some looked mean and some sad, but they all looked hungry. Dorothea wondered where they came from and who they might belong to.

She told Shadow, "I don't like seeing these poor dogs with no home." As the day went on, she decided to go feed them.

Soon, Shadow wasn't the only one following her home. About five other dogs were following too! When Dorothea got home, the pack just sat in her front yard. She would look out the window now and then, and sure enough, there they were!

After dinner, Dorothea went outside and fed them table food and led them inside the garage door. She found some old towels and made them a bed so they had a home for at least one night.

Morning came and Dorothea's mom heard dogs barking in her garage. When she opened the door, five hungry dogs were there to meet her. She just about jumped out of her shoes, but Dorothea simply walked right past and started feeding the dogs. Her mom was not too happy. Dorothea explained how they had followed her and how they needed a home.

"I just felt sorry for them," Dorothea said.

"This house is not a shelter or a kennel!" her mother replied sternly.

"I know it's not mom, but can we at least figure out a plan to help?"

"Okay, but this is your deal, young lady!"

Dorothea's mom didn't mind having dogs as guests, but she knew they needed to be adopted by good people soon. Dorothea's job was to feed, walk, and train the dogs. Her mom, in turn, would look for caring homes. Mother and daughter stapled flyers on poles and displayed them at the grocery store. The two had high hopes that people would claim the dogs, but the days went by, and there were no replies.

Dorothea kept working hard and it didn't go unnoticed. People walking down the street would stop and ask her how she got all those dogs to obey her. She would say, "I show them love and kindness, and most of the time they return the favor. Oh, one more thing, lots of doggie treats!" as she laughed.

The dogs had developed good habits, but there was one activity they just didn't want any part of, and that was taking a bath. One hot, sunny day, Dorothea filled her plastic swimming pool with water to cool herself off. At first, the dogs would come up and start drinking the water, and as they did, Dorothea would splash them. It took a few minutes, but Shadow jumped right in with her and soon they all ended up in the pool.

Dorothea's mother happened to look outside and got the biggest laugh at the sight of her daughter in a pool full of dogs. Thinking of a great idea, she ran and grabbed some shampoo bottles, rushed outside, and washed every last one of the dogs while they played with Dorothea. The yard was a mess, but all the dogs smelled really nice as the warm sun dried their fur.

14

The dogs were making great progress and Dorothea was pleased, but they couldn't stay with her family much longer. She thought, "I have different breeds here, so maybe I'd better learn more about each one."

She started to focus on their skills to help find the best possible homes. Once again, Dorothea turned to the books. She matched up the pictures to the dogs, and soon found she had a German Shepherd, a Collie, a Dalmatian, a Bloodhound, and a Chihuahua.

She told Shadow, "You're a mixed breed so you must have all kinds of skills." He only looked up and yawned, which made Dorothea smile.

Dorothea knew these breeds of dogs were really helpful in many ways. The German Shepherd helps police and military to find all kinds of things. The Collie helps on the farm by herding sheep and other animals. The Dalmatian makes a great mascot at a fire station and works well with horses. The Bloodhound has the best nose of them all and helps find missing people. Last, but not least, is the Chihuahua. They may not have very many skills, but they sure are cute and make wonderful companions.

Dorothea wanted to learn all she could. This was her way of helping and putting her skills to good use.

Dorothea made sure to check the want ads in the newspaper every day. It seemed that no one wanted a dog. However, there was a city request for anyone interested in marching in the upcoming parade. At that moment, a great idea popped into Dorothea's mind, "I'll march and so will the dogs!" She ran out the door and gathered all the dogs together.

As the dogs followed her down the street, not one stepped out of line. Her training was paying off, but she knew that simply walking down the street wouldn't be enough to make people want to adopt the dogs. Dorothea told the dogs, "We had better throw in a few good tricks to get noticed."

The tricks had to be performed on command, and the dogs would have to behave. She carried plenty of treats to feed them if they got the tricks right. Dorothea asked the dogs to dance on their hind legs and to jump up as high as they could. The Chihuahua was having a hard time so Dorothea gave him a different job instead. He was to walk out front and turn around, then give one bark to make the others jump, and two barks to make them dance. It took lots of practice, but by the day's end, the dogs were fantastic!

Dorothea made a sign for the wagon she used to carry water and treats in for the dogs. In bold letters the sign read, "Adopt a Dog Today."

As the sun came up on the day of the parade, she worked with the dogs one last time to be sure they were ready. Then they walked downtown and found their places in the parade line. As they marched, all the dogs did everything, just as planned.

The parade ended, and waiting for Dorothea was a police officer, a firefighter, a farmer, and two welcoming families. Dorothea was surprised in a happy way that all the dogs found new loving homes.

This was a happy time for Dorothea, but also very sad. She really loved each dog so much. As Dorothea started home with Shadow by her side, the mayor stopped her.

He said, "I think you did a wonderful job with those dogs, and I would like to honor you as a good citizen and role model."

Dorothea had no idea what he meant, but said, "Okay," with a smile.

One week later, Dorothea and her family were invited to city hall. The mayor presented Dorothea with a medal of achievement as the newspaper reporter took a photo of them.

The photo and story appeared in the paper the next day. Dorothea carefully cut the article from the front page and placed it in a frame. She then hung it on her wall, right next to her medal.

That evening, the local dog kennel called after reading about Dorothea in the newspaper. They asked if she could volunteer a few times a week and help out with the dogs. Her mother said it would be okay as long as she did well in school. Dorothea jumped for joy.

As Dorothea grew older, she continued to work with dogs and other animals. Her concern was always that they were healthy and happy and placed in loving homes. All of Dorothea's training and knowledge paid off, and helped her to become a veterinarian.

The city opened a dog park in her name and she grew up to be the proud owner of Dorothea's Animal Hospital and Rescue. When Dorothea looks back, she still remembers that parade and the happiness those dogs brought her. On her office wall hangs the medal and photo from that very day.

The End

Made in the USA
Monee, IL
23 December 2020